A Surprise for Mrs Magee

by Kelly Gaffney
illustrated by Lauren Mendez

a Capstone company — publishers for children

Engage Literacy is published in the UK by Raintree.
Raintree is an imprint of Capstone Global Library Limited, a company incorporated in England and Wales
having its registered office at 264 Banbury Road, Oxford, OX2 7DY – Registered company number: 6695582

www.raintree.co.uk

Text copyright © Kelly Gaffney 2021
Lead authors Jay Dale and Kelly Gaffney

Editorial credits
Erika L. Shores, editor; Kayla Rossow, designer; Laura Manthe, production specialist

A Surprise for Mrs Magee
ISBN: 978 1 4747 9937 9

Printed and bound in China.

Contents

Mum takes Mrs Magee to the shop

"Hello, Mrs Magee," called Mum from over the back fence. "Are you busy right now?"

"No, dear," replied Mrs Magee. "Can I help you with something?"

"Well," said Mum. "I'd like to buy a new plant, and I can't decide what kind to buy. Do you think you could come with me to the garden shop?"

"Oh, I'd love to," said Mrs Magee. "When would you like to go?"

"Could we go now?" asked Mum.

"I'll just get my bag," replied Mrs Magee.

"I'll meet you at the front gate," said Mum.

"Well done, Mum!" said Olivia. She was hiding behind the fence with her brother, Aiden.

"Shh!" said Mum with a smile.
"Mrs Magee and I won't be gone long.
Do you remember what you have to do?"

"Yes, Mum," replied Aiden. "I love surprises!"

"Me too!" said Olivia.

When Mrs Magee had won first prize at the garden show, she had been very excited. The children thought that they should do something to celebrate, and Olivia had come up with a great idea. She thought they could have a surprise party for Mrs Magee. Aiden said they should have it in Mrs Magee's greenhouse. After all, she really loved plants!

Mum and the children had been very busy preparing the little party. Mum had asked Mrs Magee's daughter, Anna, to come to the party, too. She lived in a different city and didn't get to see Mrs Magee very often. Mrs Magee didn't know Anna was coming, so the little party would be even more special.

BEST PLANT
1ST Place
Mrs. Magee

1ST PLACE

Anna and the children get busy

Anna had arrived early that morning. She came into the house holding some balloons. Some were shaped like flowers. The balloons were tied to green strings, and they floated in the air! Once she was inside, they began to prepare for the party.

Olivia and Aiden picked some lemons from the tree in their garden. Anna helped the children squeeze them to make a big jug of lemonade. Meanwhile, Mum baked some cupcakes. Once the cupcakes were cool, everyone put sweets on them.

They had come up with a clever plan.
Mum would take Mrs Magee out of the house
while the children set up for the party.
They decided that Mum would take
Mrs Magee to the shop. While they were
gone, Olivia, Aiden and Anna would
prepare the greenhouse and bring in the food.

Mum met Mrs Magee at the front gate.
Olivia, Aiden and Anna watched as
they drove off down the road. As soon as
they were out of sight, they quickly grabbed
the things they needed for the party.

"Let's go!" said Anna.

Anna opened the gate at the side of Mrs Magee's house. Olivia carefully carried the big jug of lemonade. The ice clinked inside the glass jug. Aiden held on tightly to the balloons. He didn't want them to float up into the sky!

Anna put a blue tablecloth on a table.
Olivia put down the heavy jug of lemonade.
One by one, they tied the balloons to the legs
of the table.

"It's very hot in here!" said Olivia.

"It sure is!" replied Anna. "Let's go and grab the cupcakes. Your mum and my mum will be back soon."

Olivia opened the greenhouse door for Aiden. He was carrying the cupcakes on a round silver tray. He carefully placed it in the middle of the table.

"Now all we have to do is wait!" said Olivia.

They bent down beside the table and waited . . . and waited . . . and waited!

Things start to warm up

"I'm so hot," groaned Aiden.

"Me too," groaned Olivia.

"I wonder what's taking them so long," said Anna.

"Oh, no!" said Olivia, as she looked inside the jug of lemonade. "All the ice is melting!"

"Oh, no!" cried Aiden. "Look at the cupcakes. The chocolate is melting, and all the sweets are slipping off!"

Just then, the balloons began to pop.

POP! POP! POP!

Aiden began to cry.

"This is terrible!" cried Olivia.

Just at that moment, they heard Mum's car pull into the driveway. The car doors closed, and they heard voices getting closer.

"That's strange," said Mrs Magee with a frown. "My gate is open."

"Perhaps the children went in to get their ball," said Mum with a smile. "I'll come in with you to check."

POP!

"What on earth is that?" said Mrs Magee. "It seems to be coming from the greenhouse!"

19

Surprise!

Mum slowly opened the greenhouse door. Mrs Magee went inside. She saw melted chocolate cupcakes and one balloon. Then she saw two sad little faces and her daughter Anna!

Pop! went the last balloon.

"Surprise," said Aiden and Olivia, sadly.

"Surprise!" said Anna. She had a big smile on her face.

"Oh, my goodness!" cried Mrs Magee.
"This is a lovely surprise!"

"I'm sorry, Mum," cried Olivia.
"I don't know why everything is going wrong!"

Mum laughed when she saw the mess
of chocolate on the tray. Then she saw
what was left of the balloons.

"I hadn't thought about how hot the
greenhouse would get!" said Mum.
"After all, it is summer!"

"Why don't we bring everything inside,"
said Mrs Magee with a smile.
"I think we will all be a lot cooler.
While we were out, I bought some ice cream.
I was hoping you could help me celebrate
winning a prize for my plant."

"That's just what we were thinking!"
laughed Mum.

Anna put her arm around Mrs Magee.
She gave her mum a big kiss on the cheek.
"Nice work, Mum!" she said. "We're so proud
of you."

Mrs Magee blushed. "My goodness. It is
very hot in here," she said with a smile.
"Let's go inside and celebrate!"

And that's just what they did!